W9-BYF-907

SIMON & SCHUSTER BOOKS FOR YOUNG READERS
An imprint of Simon & Schuster Children's Publishing Division
1230 Avenue of the Americas
New York, New York 10020

Adaptation copyright © 1998 by Simon & Schuster, Inc.
Illustrations copyright © 1998 by Simon & Schuster, Inc.

This book is based on stories previously published in RAGGEDY ANN STORIES
by Johnny Gruelle, published by Simon & Schuster.

All rights reserved including the right of reproduction in whole or in part in any form.

SIMON & SCHUSTER BOOKS FOR YOUNG READERS is a trademark of Simon & Schuster.

The text of this book is set in Fairfield.
The illustrations are rendered in Winsor and Newton ink and watercolor.
Printed and bound in the United States of America
First Edition
10 9 8 7 6 5 4 3 2

Library of Congress Cataloging-in-Publication Data
Gruelle, Johnny, 1880-1938.
        How Raggedy Ann got her candy heart / adapted from stories by Johnny Gruelle; illustrated by
Jan Palmer.
        p.   cm.
        "Adapted from the Raggedy Ann Stories."
        Summary: An accident involving a runaway kite and a can of paint threatens to
damage the doll Raggedy Ann, but ultimately it leads to her acquiring a red candy heart.
        ISBN 0-689-81119-5
        [1. Dolls—Fiction. 2. Kites—Fiction.] I. Palmer, Jan, ill. II. Gruelle, Johnny,
1880-1938. Raggedy Ann stories. III. Title.
[E]—DC20
96-26352

MY FIRST
Raggedy Ann

*How
Raggedy Ann
Got Her
Candy Heart*

*Especially for Julia —
Sunniest wishes!
Patricia Hall*

ADAPTED FROM STORIES BY
JOHNNY GRUELLE

ILLUSTRATED BY JAN PALMER

KINGSWAY
CHRISTIAN
SCHOOL
LIBRARY

SIMON & SCHUSTER BOOKS FOR YOUNG READERS

The History of Raggedy Ann

One day, a little girl named Marcella discovered an old rag doll in her attic.
Because Marcella was often ill and had to spend much of her time at home,
her father, a writer named Johnny Gruelle, looked for ways to keep her
entertained. He was inspired by Marcella's rag doll, which had bright
shoe-button eyes and red yarn hair. The doll became known as Raggedy Ann.

Knowing how much Marcella adored Raggedy Ann, Johnny Gruelle wrote
stories about the doll. He later collected the stories he had written for
Marcella and published them in a series of books. He gave Raggedy Ann a
brother, Raggedy Andy, and over the years the two rag dolls
acquired many friends.

Raggedy Ann has been an important part of Americana for more than half a
century, as well as a treasured friend to many generations of readers. After all,
she is much more than a rag doll—she is a symbol of caring and love, of
compassion and generosity. Her magical world is one that promises to delight
children of all ages for years to come.

ne day Marcella
came into the nursery.
"You're invited to a tea party,"
she told the dolls.
"We can sit outside and watch
the men painting the house."

Marcella brought all the dolls outside.
They sat in red chairs at her table
under the old apple tree.
They drank lemonade with grape jelly in it,
which made it a beautiful lavender color.
They ate cream puffs and tiny
little cookies with powdered sugar.

The sun was shining and
a soft breeze was blowing.
While Marcella and the dolls
were having their tea party,
men were painting the house.
One of the painters saw Raggedy Ann.
"Look at that rag doll," he said.
"She's a daisy."

Raggedy Ann didn't notice the painters, because she was watching some boys who were flying a kite. One boy lifted the kite above his head, while another held a ball of string. Suddenly, a breeze took the kite from the first boy.

The kite climbed high in the air. Then it fell down.

"It needs a longer tail!" one boy shouted.

"Let's tie Raggedy Ann to the tail!" Marcella suggested. "I know she would enjoy a trip way up in the sky."

The boys were delighted with this new idea. So Raggedy Ann was tied to the tail of the kite. Raggedy Ann was happy, too. She thought she might like to be up high.

This time the kite rose straight in the air, and Raggedy Ann was way, way up and far away. How Raggedy Ann enjoyed being up there! She could see for miles. The house and children were tiny, and her shoe-button eyes couldn't even spot the other dolls.

Just then there was a great puff of wind and Raggedy Ann heard a ripping sound. It was the rag that tied her to the kite.

Down below, Marcella was getting restless.
"Will you please pull the kite down now?" she asked the boys.
"I want Raggedy Ann."
The boys didn't want Raggedy Ann to come down. But the
wind puffed again and the rag tore.

Raggedy Ann went sailing
through the air as the wind caught
in her skirts. The kite began
darting and swooping to the ground.
It landed in the apple tree. And as
the boys, Marcella, and all the other dolls
watched, Raggedy Ann flew out of the sky
and fell into a can of paint!

Marcella ran to her doll. Oily, white housepaint covered
Raggedy Ann's yarn hair and her shoe-button eyes. It covered
her pretty blue dress and her striped stockings. It soaked into
her cotton stuffing.

The nice painter who liked Raggedy Ann fished her out
of the paint can. "My goodness!" he said. He looked at Marcella.
"If you let me, I'll take her home with me. I'll clean her
up tonight and bring her back."

Marcella nodded. She was too upset to speak.

The painter wrapped Raggedy Ann in newspaper. Then he brought her home and washed her in a tub.

He put her feet in the clothes wringer, and his wife
turned the crank. It was hard work, but Raggedy Ann came
through the clothes wringer. She was flat as a pancake,
and so was her smile.

The painter hung Raggedy Ann on the clothesline, and he and his wife sat down to supper.

Raggedy Ann swung upside down on the clothesline. Even after the sun went down, it was still warm outside. She wasn't lonely, because the moon and the stars kept her company.

Just before dawn, a robin and his wife flew by. They asked Raggedy Ann if they could have some of her yarn hair to line a nest for their little babies. Raggedy Ann smiled at them. They took yarn from her head and some of her cotton stuffing.

When the sun was all the way up and Raggedy Ann was quite dry and toasty warm, the painter unclipped her from the clothesline and brought her back inside.

He sewed new yarn on her hair. Then he took out the rest of her old stuffing and filled her full of fluffy new white cotton. "Don't sew her up yet," said his wife.

She pulled a paper bag from a cupboard, reached inside, and fished out a red candy heart. It had blue letters printed on it that said I LOVE YOU.

The painter took the heart from his wife. He poked it inside Raggedy Ann, just where her heart would be, and sewed her up like new. Then he said good-bye to his wife and went back to finish painting Marcella's family's house.

Marcella and the dolls had passed a sad night. They missed their friend and they wondered if they would see her again.

When the painter arrived, they were waiting under the apple tree. "Here she is," said the painter. "Fresh as a daisy." Marcella hugged Raggedy Ann. She smelled so good!

That night all the dolls arranged themselves around Raggedy Ann in the nursery, and she told them about being washed and put through the clothes wringer. She told them about Mama and Papa Robin and about being dried and stuffed and made just like new. Last of all, she told them about the candy heart that read I LOVE YOU.